5/19

D1217612

The AMAZING ADVENTURES of BATMAN™

MUD MENACE!

by **Laurie S. Sutton**

illustrated by **Dario Brizuela**

Batman created by Bob Kane with Bill Finger

PICTURE WINDOW BOOKS
a capstone imprint

The Amazing Adventures of Batman
is published by Picture Window Books
A Capstone Imprint
1710 Roe Crest Drive
North Mankato, Minnesota 56003
www.mycapstone.com

STAR41051

Cataloging-in-Publication Data is available on the Library of Congress website.
ISBN: 978-1-5158-3979-8 (library binding)
ISBN: 978-1-5158-3984-2 (eBook PDF)

Summary: When Clayface robs the Gotham City Museum, Batman and
Ace the Bat-Hound team up to take down the . . . Mud Menace!

Editor: Christopher Harbo
Designer: Kayla Rossow

Printed in the United States of America.
PA49

TABLE OF CONTENTS

Mud Night at the Museum **7**

Mud Fight **14**

All Washed Up **21**

Batman's Secret Message! **28**

Hidden in the shadows,
a hero keeps watch.
He is the Caped Crusader
against crime. He is the
Dark Knight of justice.
These are ...

The **AMAZING ADVENTURES** of
BATMAN

Chapter 1
MUD NIGHT AT THE MUSEUM

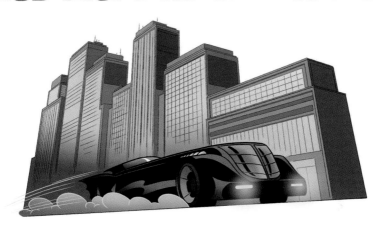

Batman patrols Gotham

City in the Batmobile. By his

side sits Ace the Bat-Hound.

Suddenly a police alert

comes over the Batmobile's

radio. **BEEP! BEEP! BEEP!**

"Calling all units! The
Gotham City Museum is
being robbed!" a voice on
the radio says.

The Dark Knight speeds toward the Gotham City Museum. He and Ace find the museum surrounded by police and firefighters.

Police Commissioner James Gordon walks up to Batman and Ace.

"All the alarms in the museum went off at once," Gordon tells Batman. "We know a robbery is taking place inside, but we don't know where."

"Ace and I will find out," the Dark Knight says.

"Arf! Arf!" Ace agrees.

The super heroes run into

the museum. They quickly

find muddy footprints. Ace

tracks them to the villain.

"Clayface!" Batman says.

The villain holds a large,

pink jewel in his hand. He

swallows the gem and then

leaps at the heroes.

Clayface turns his hands
into hammers. He tries to
smack Batman and Ace.

WHACK! WHAAAACK!

The heroes dodge the
villain's blows.

Chapter 2

MUD FIGHT

Clayface changes his

attack. He starts to throw

things at Batman and Ace.

The objects are priceless

pieces of art.

While the heroes catch

vases and statues, Clayface

runs into the Dinosaur

Hall. A giant model of a

Tyrannosaurus rex gives

him an idea.

Moments later, Batman
and Ace dash into the
Dinosaur Hall.

ROAAAR!

Clayface has turned into
a giant, muddy T. rex!

Ace chomps the T. rex's tail. Clayface whips his tail to shake Ace loose, but the Bat-Hound hangs on.

Batman tosses a Batrope around the mud monster's neck. He uses it to leap onto the T. rex's back. Clayface tries to buck Batman off.

"It's like riding a bucking bronco," Batman says.

The Dark Knight throws another Batrope around the T. rex's snout. He uses it to guide the monster through the museum.

Batman steers Clayface
toward the museum's front
doors. Ace bounces along on
the clay dinosaur's tail.

"Hang on," the Dark
Knight calls out.

STOMP! STOMP! STOMP!

They lumber through the doors. The heroes ride the T. rex down the museum's steps and onto the street.

Chapter 3

ALL WASHED UP

Batman turns the clay

T. rex toward the police cars

and fire trucks. The flashing

lights confuse the monster.

Clayface spins in circles.

Ace still hangs onto the T. rex's tail. At the same time, he uses one paw to shoot a Bat-Grapnel from his Utility Collar.

THWOOONK! The grapnel sinks into the base of the museum.

"Arf! Arf!" Ace barks as he lets go of the T. rex's tail and circles the villain's legs.

The Batrope attached to

the grapnel wraps around

Clayface's dinosaur legs.

SPLAAAT! The T. rex falls

flat on his back.

Batman jumps off the
dinosaur as the firefighters
spray their water hoses.

"No!" the villain cries as
they melt him down.

Then the police rush up

with super-sized vacuums.

VROOOM! VROOOM!

They suck up Clayface in

his liquid form.

The stolen jewel glitters on the street. Ace fetches the gem and brings it to the Dark Knight.

"Good boy!" Batman says. Then he hands the jewel to Commissioner Gordon.

"Thank you for saving the gem, Batman," Gordon says. "And thank you, Ace, for another doggone amazing adventure!"

BATMAN'S SECRET MESSAGE!

Hey, kids! What was Clayface before he became a super-villain?

1
16 18 15 6 5 19 19 9 15 14 1 12
1 3 20 15 18

Use the code below to solve the Batcomputer's secret message!

1	2	3	4	5	6	7	8	9	10	11	12	13
A	B	C	D	E	F	G	H	I	J	K	L	M

14	15	16	17	18	19	20	21	22	23	24	25	26
N	O	P	Q	R	S	T	U	V	W	X	Y	Z

alert (uh-LURT)—a warning of danger

bronco (BRAHNG-ko)—a wild horse

commissioner (kuh-MI-shuh-nuhr)—an official who heads up a government agency

grapnel (GRAP-nuhl)—a grappling hook

patrol (puh-TROHL)—to protect and watch an area

priceless (PRISSE-liss)—relating to something too precious to put a value on

surround (suh-ROUND)—to be on every side of something

villain (VIL-uhn)—a wicked, evil, or bad person who is often a character in a story

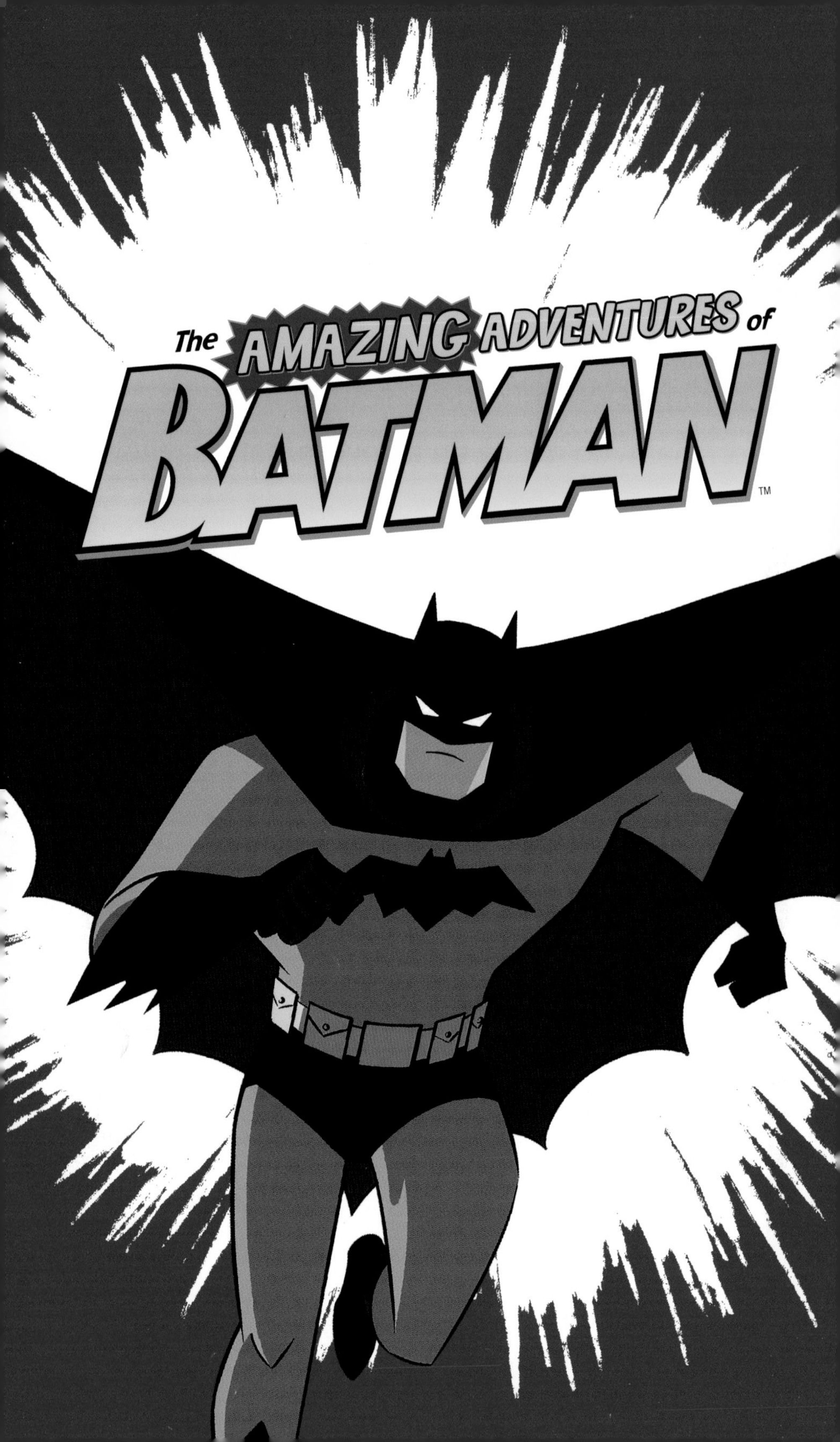
The AMAZING ADVENTURES of
BATMAN™

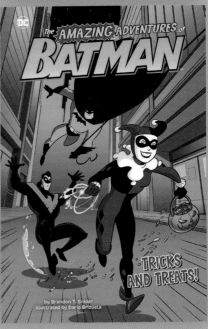

COLLECT THEM ALL!

only from . . . **PICTURE WINDOW BOOKS**

Author

Laurie S. Sutton has read comics since she was a kid. She grew up to become an editor for Marvel, DC Comics, Starblaze, and Tekno Comics. She has written for series such as Adam Strange for DC, Star Trek: Voyager for Marvel, and Star Trek: Deep Space Nine and Witch Hunter for Malibu Comics. There are long boxes of comics in her closet where there should be clothing and shoes. Laurie has lived all over the world, and currently resides in Florida.

Illustrator

Dario Brizuela was born in Buenos Aires, Argentina in 1977. He enjoys doing illustration work and character design for several companies including DC Comics, Marvel Comics, Image Comics, IDW Publishing, Titan Publishing, Hasbro, Capstone Publishers, and Disney Publishing Worldwide. Dario's work can be found in a wide range of properties including Star Wars Tales, Ben 10, DC Super Friends, Justice League Unlimited, Batman: The Brave & The Bold, Transformers, Teenage Mutant Ninja Turtles, Batman 66, Wonder Woman 77, Teen Titans Go!, Scooby Doo! Team Up, and DC Super Hero Girls.